Pug's Got Talent

Read all the Diary of a Pug books!

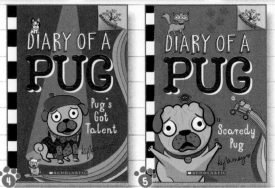

More books coming soon!

DIARY OF A PUG

PUG

Pug's Got Talent

By Kyla May

BRANCHES

SCHOLASTIC INC.

To Bear, my inspiration. You captured my heart and my imagination.

Special thanks to Sonia Sander

© Art copyright © 2021 by Kyla May Dinsmore
Text copyright © 2021 by Scholastic Inc.

Photos © KylaMay2019

Library of Congress Cataloging-in-Publication Data Available

ISBN 9781338530131 (reinforced library binding) / ISBN 9781338530124 (pb)

10 9 8 7 6 5 4 3 2 1   21 22 23 24 25

Printed in China   62
First edition, February 2021
Edited by Katie Woehr
Book design by Kyla May and Christian Zelaya

Table of Contents

Chapter 1

SHOW DOG

SATURDAY

Dear Diary,

BVB here. That's **BARON VON BUBBLES**. But everyone calls me BUB.

Wait until you hear my show-stopping news!

But first, here are some things to know about me:

I have a passion for fashion.

I make many different faces:

Naptime Face

Splashed with Water Face

Nervous Face (or I Just Farted Face)

Here are some of my favorite things:

MY SKATEBOARD

PEANUT BUTTER TREATS

MY BEST FRIEND

LUNA

Here are some things that get on my nerves:

DUCHESS

NUTZ

And **WATER**! That's right! I still don't like water!

Bella laughed so hard the first time I jumped into a bubble bath. I had no idea there was WATER under the bubbles! (That's how I got my name, by the way.)

Now back to my show-stopping news! On our walk today, Bella told me about a block party that will take place in front of our house next Saturday.

They close off the street to all cars. There are games, food, and music. It's like a fair. This year, I said I'd host a talent show. But I need a theme. Like show tunes or cool stunts!

Stunts?! I love stunts! They come in handy for jumping over puddles.

Bella saw my stunt. She stopped and scooped me up.

You just gave me the best idea for the talent show! We'll get started tomorrow. Jack and Luna can help!

I gave you an idea?!

Chapter 2

SHOWBIZ

SUNDAY

Dear Diary,

I had to wait until we were all in Jack and Luna's tree fort to hear Bella's idea.

> Drumroll, please. We'll do a... <u>PET</u> TALENT SHOW!

A pet talent show sounded awesome!

It's a great idea!

It WOULD be great if any of you had any talent.

Um, have you seen me skateboard?

Then Bella said something super exciting.

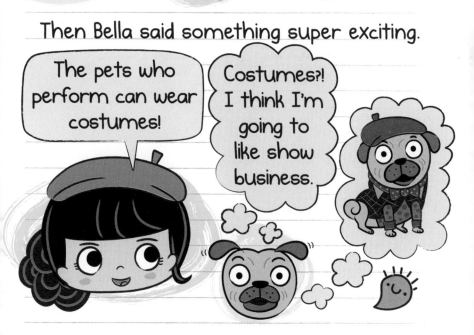

The pets who perform can wear costumes!

Costumes?! I think I'm going to like show business.

We started planning right away.

We made flyers. I helped.

Pet Talent
Show 🐾
Auditions
TOMORROW!
🐾 4:00 PM
Bella's House

Paint

We handed the flyers out to our neighbors. Some of the pets weren't as excited about the idea as their humans.

I didn't agree to this.

I'm doing it because I love Bella. And costumes.

Come on, Pippa. Do it for your girl!

Other pets couldn't wait for the auditions!

But their humans needed convincing.

Tonight I was pooped from giving out flyers. But as tired as I was, I couldn't fall asleep. Neither could Bella.

Chapter 3

SHOW AND TELL

MONDAY

Dear Diary,

All four of us were nervous as Jack and Bella headed off to school. Bella tried to lighten the mood by asking about Luna's act.

What will Luna do?

It's a surprise.

I love surprises!

Me too!

After school, the line of pets waiting to audition was all the way down the block!

I guess we didn't have to be worried about people not showing up.

Talent Show AUDITIONS

Of course, nosy Nutz had to find out what was going on.

Bella and Jack got the auditions started.

Luna and I helped.

We loved the puppies' act.

Little Kitty was next. I was impressed by her high-wire act. Duchess wasn't.

Is that it? A catwalk?

I don't see YOU up there.

A few acts didn't go well.

Then guess what happened, Diary? Nutz tried to get in the show!

Is that a drumming squirrel?

What? Where?

Nice try, Nutz!

I've got talent, too!

PETS only!

That was a close one, Diary. Can you imagine the trouble he would have caused?!

Bella and Jack will choose which pets will be in the show and put up a list tomorrow. I can't wait to see who I will share the stage with!

Chapter 4

SHOW LINEUP

TUESDAY

Dear Diary,

Bella and I got up early to hang up the list of acts.

BLOCK PARTY PET TALENT SHOW

Performing Pets:
...oarding
...e Dutch
...arachuting
...t
...ncing
... Peanut
...eats
...nesday 4p.m.
...rsday 4p.m.
...nt Show: Saturday 4p.m.

BLOCK PARTY PET TALENT SHOW

 **Performing Pets:**

1. Bub: Skateboarding
2. Pippa: Hula-Hoop
3. Kitty: High-Wire
4. Bitty Birds: Flying
5. Border Collie: Double Dutch
6. Gilly Guinea Pig: Parachuting
7. Luna: Surprise Act
8. Petunia Pig: Tap Dancing
9. Puppies: Balancing Peanut
           Butter Treats

First rehearsal: Wednesday 4p.m.

Dress rehearsal: Friday 4p.m.

Pet Talent Show: Saturday 4p.m.

As Bella and Jack headed to school, they reminded us to practice our acts.

Four days until the show. Make sure you practice!

3. Kitty: High-Wire
4. Bitty Birds: Flying
5. Border Collie: Double tch
6. Gilly Guinea Pig: Parad uting
7. Luna: Surprise Act
8. Petunia Pig: Tap Dancing
9. Puppies: B

But Luna, don't let Bub see your act. Don't spoil the surprise!

It's driving me crazy not knowing what Luna's act is. Practicing my stunts helped me forget for awhile.

Then Duchess showed up.

But Duchess never leaves me alone.
She pointed out every wrong move
I made.

You're never going to land that flip.

You think you can do better?

I <u>know</u> I can. Get ready...

Diary, you won't believe this. Duchess nailed the flip.

I couldn't believe Duchess was so good at acrobatics.

Why didn't you try out for the show?

Because I would outshine all of you!

As Duchess proudly marched away, I heard a sound from Luna's backyard.

SPLASH!

Will Luna be using WATER in her act?

I have a bad feeling about this, Diary!

Chapter 5

SHOWSTOPPER

WEDNESDAY

Dear Diary,

  We had our first rehearsal today. ("Rehearsal" means "practice run" in showbiz talk.) I went first and did my act onstage. Everything went perfectly!

Then it was the puppies' turn. I still loved their act. Someone else loved it, too.

Woooo-hoooo!

What are you up to, Nutz?

Just cheering on a good act!

I needed to keep an eye on Nutz. But it was time for Luna's act. I couldn't miss the surprise!

I looked where Nutz was pointing...and I did NOT like what I saw.

Jack and Luna were pulling out a kiddie pool and a ladder. Luna was going to do a high-dive into the pool! That meant lots of WATER!

I rushed out of the splash zone and under the stage just in time. Guess who was hiding under there?

Oh no. Did Bubby-kins almost get wet?

Look who's talking. You were hiding here first.

Then it hit me. For not wanting to be in the show, Duchess was hanging around A LOT. I wanted some answers.

Why ARE you here? You said you didn't want to be in the show.

I never said that. I would have auditioned. But nobody asked me.

I know it's hard to believe, but Duchess has feelings! And her feelings were hurt.

You and Bella always forget about me when you do fun things.

That was true, Diary. We often did things without Duchess.

I had no idea you wanted to do stuff with us, Duchess. I'm sorry.

I never thought I'd say this, but I would like to help Duchess. Maybe I can get her in the show. I will make a plan tomorrow.

Chapter 6

SHOW-OFF

THURSDAY

Dear Diary,

This morning, I made a plan to get Duchess in the show. But helping her wasn't easy! We are NOT used to being nice to each other.

If you really want to be in the show, I can help you.

Help!? From you!?

Okay. Never mind...

Well, if you're going to beg me, I'll do it.

As Bella headed to school, I put my plan into action. Duchess would be in my act with me. I started to show her where she could jump in.

It turned out Duchess already knew my whole act! She had a few ideas of her own.

Duchess's ideas were good, but it started to feel like Duchess was the star of MY act.

I wondered if I had made a mistake inviting Duchess to be in my act. What if everyone watches her instead of me, Diary? But the act IS more exciting now, and Duchess seems so happy.

That was your best move yet, Bubby-kins.

Was that a compliment?!

Maybe. Don't get used to it.

We finished practicing just as Bella came home. Duchess kept walking in circles. She does that when she's nervous.

We will show Bella the new act tomorrow.

Are you sure this is going to work?

Don't you trust me?

Not usually. But I will try in this case.

Gee, thanks.

I needed a break from Duchess then, so I went to see what Bella was up to.

She was sewing my costume!

Oh, Bubby.
You will be the best
dressed act of all!

My costume <u>did</u> look stunning. But I realized something... Bella had not made a costume for Duchess, because she didn't know Duchess would be performing! Our act would look silly if only one of us had a costume!

I had to fix this. I waited for Bella to fall asleep. Then I snuck over to the scrap pile. Maybe I could make Duchess an outfit.

A little of this…a little of that…

But I was tired and the scrap pile was so comfy.

I'll just rest my eyes for a moment…

Chapter 7

THE SHOW MUST GO ON

FRIDAY

Dear Diary,

Today was dress rehearsal. ("Dress rehearsal" is showbiz for "practice run <u>with costumes</u>.") But I fell asleep in the scrap pile last night! Duchess still didn't have a costume! Or so I thought…

I put on my costume, too. I hated to admit it, but Duchess and I looked amazing together.

We practiced all day. The act was flawless!

When Bella and Jack got home, it was time for dress rehearsal to start. All the performers gathered backstage. For some reason, Nutz was there, too.

Duchess and I waited backstage for Bella to introduce my act. This was it—how would Bella react to Duchess's surprise appearance? I rolled onstage when Bella called my name.

Here's Bub!

I did a stunt, rolled offstage, and picked up Duchess. Then we both rolled back onstage.

Huh? What's Duchess doing in Bubby's act?

And WHAT is Duchess wearing?!

I waited for Duchess to do her triple flip. But she didn't move. She was FROZEN in place!

Just then, the puppies ran across the stage. Nutz was chasing them!

The chase made Duchess snap out of her daze. She freaked out and ran offstage.

R-R-R-O-O-W-W-W!

Duchess was so freaked out, she ran into Luna's ladder. It fell over and hit the pool.

The stage was flooded. There was no way we could practice the rest of the show. Bella sent everyone home.

I'm sorry most of you could not rehearse tonight. We'll see you here for the show tomorrow.

Bella was worried as we cleaned the stage. I felt awful.

Duchess joining your act sure caused a mess, Bubby. I hope nothing goes wrong tomorrow.

I'll make sure nothing does.

Later, I searched for Duchess. I wanted to understand what happened to her onstage. But I couldn't find her.

I did find Nutz, though.

Hey. What was all that chasing about?

The puppies and I were just playing. Can't I make friends?

I don't buy it, Diary. That squirrel is up to something. I guess we'll find out at the show tomorrow . . .

Chapter 8

SHOWTIME

SATURDAY

Dear Diary,

Today was the block party, and it was finally SHOWTIME! The stage was back in order. The pets were dressed and ready. (None of them looked as snazzy as me.) Luckily, Nutz was nowhere to be seen. I still couldn't find Duchess. Would I have to do the act alone?

Places, everyone!

I peeked out from behind the curtain.
There were a lot of people in the audience.
I got a little nervous. All of a sudden,
Duchess appeared.

Feeling nervous, stinker?

Duchess! Where
have you been?
What happened
yesterday?

Her answer surprised me. It was an apology!

I'm sorry. I got scared to do my tricks in front of everyone.

I was speechless, Diary. Duchess had stage fright?! But she is the queen of confidence.

You should do the act without me. You'll be great! Break a leg!
What?! That's mean!
"Break a leg" means "good luck" in showbiz, silly.
Oh. I knew that. Thanks.

Bella called my name a moment later. I went onstage and zipped and flipped. I missed Duchess, but I nailed all my tricks.

The rest of the show was fabulous. I even stayed dry during Luna's high-dive! We were down to our final act—the puppies and their treats.

The puppies' act was awesome. But halfway through, Duchess pointed to something. Nutz!

Of course he was, Diary. We had to stop him before he ruined the show!

I told her my plan. Then I grabbed
my skateboard.

Duchess landed as the puppies finished. It was like we were always part of their act! We saved the treats AND the show. The crowd went wild.

After the show, we all celebrated together.

That was the best pet talent show ever!

You did it, Duchess! You got over your stage fright!

Me? Stage fright? Never. You must have been dreaming, Bubby-kins.

Oh Diary, that cat gets on my nerves! But you know what? We are already planning our act for next year. We might even ask Nutz to join us!

Kyla May

Kyla May is an Australian illustrator, writer, and designer. In addition to books, Kyla creates animation. She lives by the beach in Victoria, Australia, with her three daughters and two pups. The character of Bub was inspired by her daughter's pug called Bear.

HOW MUCH DO YOU KNOW ABOUT

DIARY OF A PUG

Pug's Got Talent?

What gives me the idea for a pet talent show?

When Bella first shares her idea for a pet talent show, Bub is excited to do his stunts. Why else is Bub excited about the show?

Why does Bub run to hide when I go onstage to practice my act?

When Duchess is frozen onstage, what snaps her out of her daze?

If you were performing in a talent show, what talent would you show off? Draw a picture of yourself performing. Don't forget your costume!

scholastic.com/branches